THE BOOK OF

TOY
stories

For Edmund
L.C.

For Sara
E.C.C.

KINGFISHER
An imprint of Kingfisher Publications Plc
New Penderel House, 283-288 High Holborn, London WC1V 7HZ
www.kingfisherpub.com

First published in hardback by Kingfisher 2000
First published in paperback by Kingfisher 2001
2 4 6 8 10 9 7 5 3 1
1TR/0901/MID/RNB(FR)/140MA

ACKNOWLEDGEMENTS

The publisher would like to thank the copyright holders for permission to reproduce the following copyright material:

Ruth Ainsworth: Egmont Children's Books Limited, London for "Jack-in-the-Box" from *The Pirate Ship and Other Stories* by Ruth Ainsworth, published by William Heinemann Ltd 1951. Copyright © Ruth Ainsworth 1951. **Aingelda Ardizzone:** Laura Cecil Literary Agency for "The Little Girl and the Tiny Doll" by Aingelda Ardizzone. Copyright © Aingelda Ardizzone 1966. **Hans Christian Andersen:** Andersen Press Ltd for "The Steadfast Tin Soldier" from *The Flying Trunk and Other Stories* by Hans Christian Andersen, retold by Naomi Lewis, published by Andersen Press Ltd. Copyright © Naomi Lewis 1986. **Joyce Lankester Brisley:** Kingfisher Publications Plc. for "Adventure in the Garden" from *Adventures of Purl and Plain* by Joyce Lankester Brisley, published by George G. Harrap & Co. Ltd. 1941. Copyright © Joyce Lankester Brisley 1941. **Johnny Gruelle:** "Raggedy Ann Rescues Fido". All trademarks of Raggedy Ann (including the original illustrations by Johnny Gruelle) are property of Simon & Schuster, Inc. **Irina Hale:** Laura Cecil Literary Agency for "Brown Bear in a Brown Chair". Copyright © Irina Hale 1983. **Russell Hoban:** David Higham Associates Ltd for "The Tin Horseman" from *La Corona and the Tin Frog and Other Tales* by Russell Hoban, published by Jonathan Cape 1979. The story first appeared in Puffin Annual 1974. Copyright © Russell Hoban 1974. **E.T.A. Hoffmann:** "The Nutcracker" by E.T.A. Hoffmann, retold by Vivian French. Copyright © Vivian French 2000.

Every effort has been made to obtain permission to reproduce copyright material but there may be cases where we have been unable to contact a copyright holder. The publisher will be happy to correct any omissions in future printings.

THE
KINGFISHER BOOK OF
TOY
stories

Compiled by Laura Cecil

Illustrated by Emma Chichester Clark

KING*f*ISHER

Contents

Brown Bear
in a Brown Chair

IRINA HALE

 There once was a Brown Bear who
lived in a brown chair. He was sat
upon very often, because you couldn't see
he was there.

"I'm feeling so flat," he said, "when really
a bear should feel happy and fat."

One day, he had a good idea, so he called
Maggie, the little girl whose Bear he was.

"I must have a ribbon round my neck," he said, "so that people can see I'm here."

Maggie got him a yellow ribbon off a chocolate box.

Bear sat happily on his chair.

A mother bird on the windowsill saw him.

She cheeped to her children, "Look! There's a bear in that room with no clothes on! Only a yellow ribbon round his neck, and nothing else!"

Bear began to feel he was wearing too little.

"I hope those nasty birds don't find any worms for breakfast today," he said.

"I have to have some trousers now," Bear told Maggie. So she cut the legs off an old pair of stripey pants to Bear's size and hemmed them.

But they were too tight and made his tummy stick out.

Suddenly Bear saw a little mouse, peeping at him over the chair.

It squeaked, "Oh what a fat, lazy bear! Just lying around on a chair all day! Not like us poor mice. We have to work hard just to find one tiny crumb!"

So Bear said to Maggie, "Now I must have a shirt, to cover my tummy that's sticking out!"

Maggie sat down and made him a shirt, sewing with large stitches. It took a bit of time, but at last, there it was, finished.

Bear felt very proud.

"Aren't I well-dressed?" Bear said.

Just then, the cat went by and said, "How can you be well-dressed if you don't have shoes on? Bears like you don't deserve to sit on comfy armchairs!" (The cat really wanted the chair all to himself.)

Bear stamped his feet till Maggie came. "I've got to have a pair of shoes now, or I'll never be really well-dressed."

So Maggie had to take the shoes off her doll for Bear.

The doll was very cross and gave a big sneeze.

"I shall get a bad cold now, all because of you!" she said to Bear. But he pretended not to hear.

"Am I dressed right, now?" Bear said to the poodle who was watching him. He stood on his head, feet up, to show off his new shoes.

The poodle sniffed. "You can't be in fashion without a hat! Didn't you know? All smart people have hats!"

So Bear wanted a hat next.

But what excuse could he find this time?

"Maggie!" he said.

"I feel cold on my head . . ."

Maggie looked at him and went off to find a little sunhat in the bottom of a drawer. She had worn it when she was a baby. It was just Bear's size.

"There, is that all now?" she asked, putting his hat on. "You are really becoming quite a Bothersome Bear!"

Bear sat with his hat on, thinking hard. What else was there that he must have and didn't have?

Just then the parrot woke up on his perch. He fixed a wicked eye on Bear. Suddenly he screeched, "You do look silly! Just like a clown dressed up for the circus!"

Bear was very upset.

Though he was all dressed up, he only made people laugh!

Then he had his second good idea – to throw off all those horrid clothes quickly! They were making him feel very uncomfortable and not at all like himself.

Up went his hat into the air. Off with those tight trousers! Shoes – away with them – one, two! He felt better and better

every minute! The shirt and the ribbon went last. All the animals cheered.

Maggie's mother made a new cover for the old brown chair.

Bear said, "A brown bear shows up well on a flowery chair. I won't be sat on by mistake any more!"

But there was a bit of leftover flowery material. Maggie's mother made Bear a little dress out of it.

So there he was again, a bear wearing the same pattern as the chair. And everyone was sure to sit on him as before.

Raggedy Ann Rescues Fido

JOHNNY GRUELLE

It was almost midnight and the dolls were asleep in their beds; all except Raggedy Ann.

Raggedy lay there, her shoe-button eyes staring straight up at the ceiling. Every once in a while Raggedy Ann ran her rag hand up through her yarn hair. She was thinking.

When she had thought for a long, long time, Raggedy Ann raised herself on her wobbly elbows and said, "I've thought it all out."

At this the other dolls shook each other and raised up saying, "Listen! Raggedy has thought it all out!"

"Tell us what you have been thinking, dear Raggedy," said the tin soldier. "We hope they were pleasant thoughts."

"Not very pleasant thoughts!" said Raggedy, as she brushed a tear from her shoe-button eyes. "You haven't seen Fido all day, have you?"

"Not since early this morning," the French dolly said.

"It has troubled me," said Raggedy, "and if my head was not stuffed with lovely new white cotton, I am sure it would have ached with the worry! When Mistress took me into the living-room this afternoon she was crying, and I heard her mamma say, 'We will find him! He is sure to come home soon!' and I knew they were talking of Fido! He must be lost!"

The tin soldier jumped out of bed and ran over to Fido's basket, his tin feet clicking on the floor as he went. "He is not here," he said.

"When I was sitting in the window about noontime," said the Indian doll, "I saw Fido and a yellow scraggly dog playing out on the lawn and they ran out through a hole in the fence!"

"That was Priscilla's dog, Peterkins!" said the French doll.

"I know poor Mistress is very sad on account of Fido," said the Dutch doll, "because I was in the dining-room at suppertime and I heard her daddy tell her to eat her supper and he would go out and find Fido; but I had forgotten all about it until now."

"That is the trouble with all of us except Raggedy Ann!" cried the little penny doll, in a squeaky voice. "She has to think for all of us!"

"I think it would be a good plan for us to show our love for Mistress and try and find Fido!" exclaimed Raggedy.

"It is a good plan, Raggedy Ann!" cried all the dolls. "Tell us how to start about it."

"Well, first let us go out upon the lawn and see if we can track the dogs!" said Raggedy.

"I can track them easily!" the Indian doll said, "for Indians are good at trailing things!"

"Then let us waste no more

time in talking!" said Raggedy Ann, as she jumped from bed, followed by the rest.

The nursery window was open, so the dolls helped each other up on the sill and then jumped to the soft grass below. They fell in all sorts of queer attitudes, but of course the fall did not hurt them.

At the hole in the fence the Indian doll picked up the trail of the two dogs, and the dolls, stringing out behind, followed him until they came to Peterkins' house. Peterkins was surprised to see the strange little figures in white nighties come stringing up the path to the dog-house.

Peterkins was too large to sleep in the nursery, so he had a nice cosy dog-house under the grape arbour.

"Come in," Peterkins said when he saw and recognized the dolls, so all the dollies went into Peterkins' house and sat about while Raggedy told him why they had come.

"It has worried me, too!" said Peterkins. "But I had no way of telling your mistress where Fido was, for she cannot understand dog language! For you see," Peterkins continued, "Fido and I were having the grandest romp over in the park when a great big man with a funny thing on the end of a stick came running towards us. We barked at him and Fido thought he was trying to play with us and went up too close and do you know, that wicked man caught Fido in the thing at the end of the stick and carried him to a wagon and dumped him in with a lot of other dogs!"

"*The Dog Catcher!*" cried Raggedy Ann.

"Yes!" said Peterkins, as he wiped his eyes with his paws. "It was the dog catcher! For I followed the wagon at a distance and I saw him put all the dogs into a big wire pen, so that none could get out!"

"Then you know the way there, Peterkins?" asked Raggedy Ann.

"Yes, I can find it easily," Peterkins said.

"Then show us the way,"

Raggedy Ann cried, "for we must try to rescue Fido!"

So Peterkins led the way up alleys and across streets, the dolls all pattering along behind him. It was a strange procession. Once a strange dog ran out at them, but Peterkins told him to mind his own business and the strange dog returned to his own yard.

At last they came to the dog catcher's place. Some of the dogs in the pen were barking at the moon and others were whining and crying.

There was Fido, all covered with mud, and his pretty red ribbon dragging on the ground. My, but he was glad to see the dolls and Peterkins! All the dogs came to the side of the pen and twisted their heads from side to side, gazing in wonder at the queer figures of the dolls.

"We will try and let you out," said Raggedy Ann.

At this all the dogs barked joyfully.

Then Raggedy Ann, the other dolls and Peterkins went to the gate.

The catch was too high for Raggedy Ann to reach, but Peterkins held Raggedy Ann in his mouth and stood up on his hind legs so that she could raise the catch.

When the catch was raised, the dogs were so anxious to get out they pushed and jumped against the gate so hard it flew open, knocking Peterkins and Raggedy Ann into the mud. Such a yapping and barking was never heard in the neighbourhood as when the dogs swarmed out of the enclosure, jumping over one another and scrambling about in the mad rush out of the gate.

Fido picked himself up from where he had been rolled by the large dogs and helped Raggedy Ann to her feet. He, Peterkins, and

all the dolls ran after the pack of dogs, turning the corner just as the dog catcher came running out of the house in his nightgown to see what was causing the trouble.

He stopped in astonishment when he saw the string of dolls in white nighties pattering down the alley, for he could not imagine what they were.

Well, you may be sure the dolls thanked Peterkins for his kind assistance and they and Fido ran on home, for a faint light was beginning to show in the east where the sun was getting ready to come up.

When they got to their own home they found an old chair out in the yard and after a great deal of work they finally dragged it to the window and thus managed to get into the nursery again.

Fido was very grateful to Raggedy Ann and the other dolls and before he went to his basket he gave them each a lick on the cheek.

The dolls lost no time in scrambling into bed and pulling up the covers, for they were very sleepy, but just as they were dozing off, Raggedy Ann raised herself and said, "If my legs and arms were not stuffed with nice clean cotton I feel sure they would ache, but being stuffed with nice clean white cotton, they do not ache and I could not feel happier if my body was stuffed with sunshine, for I know how pleased and happy Mistress will be in the morning when she discovers Fido asleep in his own little basket, safe and sound at home."

And as the dollies by this time were all asleep, Raggedy Ann pulled the sheet up to her chin and smiled so hard she ripped two stitches out of the back of her rag head.

The Steadfast Tin Soldier

HANS CHRISTIAN ANDERSEN
RETOLD BY NAOMI LEWIS

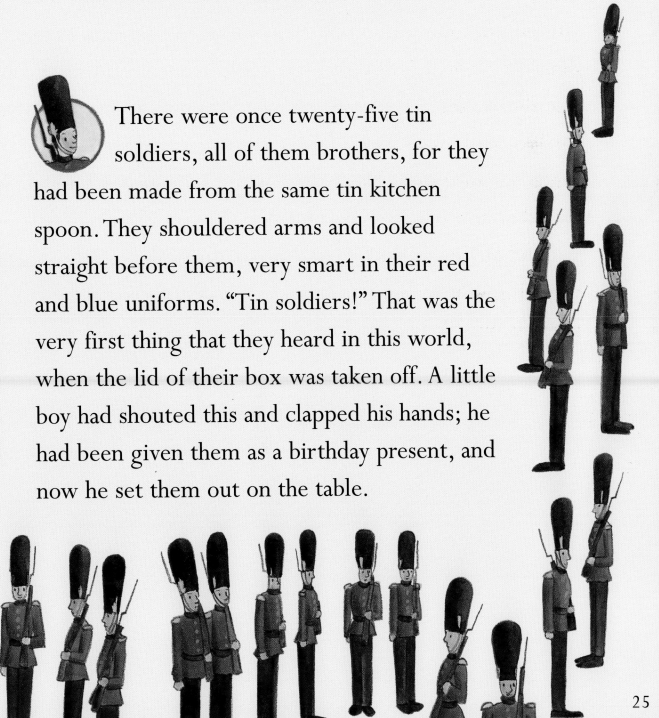

There were once twenty-five tin soldiers, all of them brothers, for they had been made from the same tin kitchen spoon. They shouldered arms and looked straight before them, very smart in their red and blue uniforms. "Tin soldiers!" That was the very first thing that they heard in this world, when the lid of their box was taken off. A little boy had shouted this and clapped his hands; he had been given them as a birthday present, and now he set them out on the table.

Each soldier was exactly like the next – except for one, which had only a single leg; he was the last to be moulded, and there was not quite enough tin left. Yet he stood just as well on his one leg as the others did on their two, and he is this story's hero.

On the table where they were placed there were many other toys, but the one which everyone noticed first was a paper castle. Through its little windows you could see right into the rooms. In front of it, tiny trees were arranged round a piece of mirror, which was meant to look like a lake. Swans made of wax seemed to float on its surface, and gaze at their white reflections. The whole scene was enchanting – and the prettiest thing of all was a girl who stood in the open doorway; she too was cut out of paper, but her gauzy skirt was of finest muslin; a narrow blue ribbon crossed her shoulder like a scarf, and was held by a shining sequin almost the size of her face. This charming little creature held both of her arms stretched out, for she was a dancer; indeed, one of her legs was raised so high in the air that the tin soldier could not see it at all; he thought that she had only one leg like himself.

"Now she would be just the right wife for me," he thought. "But she is so grand; she lives in a castle, and I have only a box – and there are five-and-twenty of us in that! There certainly isn't room for her. Still, I can try to make her acquaintance." So he lay down full length behind a snuff-box which was on the table; from there he could easily watch the little paper dancer, who continued to stand on one leg without losing her balance.

When evening came, all the other tin soldiers were put in their box, and the children went to bed. Now the toys began to have games of their own; they played at visiting, and schools, and battles, and going to parties. The tin soldiers rattled in their box, for they wanted to join in, but they couldn't get the lid off. The nutcrackers turned somersaults, and the slate pencil squeaked on the slate; there was such a din that the canary woke up and took part in the talk – what's more, he did it in verse. The only two who didn't move were the tin soldier and the little dancer; she continued to stand on the point of her toe, with her arms held out; he stood just as steadily on his single leg – and never once did he take his eyes from her.

Now the clock struck twelve. Crack! – the snuff-box lid flew open and up hopped a little goblin. There was no snuff in the box – it was a kind of trick, a jack-in-the-box.

"Tin soldier!" screeched the goblin. "Keep your eyes to yourself!"

But the tin soldier pretended not to hear.

"All right, just you wait till tomorrow!" said the goblin.

When morning came and the children were up again, the tin soldier was placed on the window ledge. The goblin may have been responsible, or perhaps a draught blowing through – anyhow, the window suddenly swung open, and out fell the tin soldier, all the three storeys to the ground. It was a frightful fall! His leg pointed upwards, his head was down, and he came to a halt with his bayonet stuck between the paving stones.

The servant-girl and the little boy went to search in the street, but although they were almost treading on the soldier they somehow failed to see him. If he had called out, "Here I am!" they would have found him easily, but he didn't think it proper behaviour to cry out when he was in uniform.

Now it began to rain; the drops fell fast – it was a drenching shower. When it was over, a pair of urchins passed. "Look!" said one of them. "There's a tin soldier. Let's put him out to sea."

So they made a boat out of newspaper and put the tin soldier in the middle, and set it in the fast-flowing gutter at the edge of the street. Away he sped, and the two boys ran beside him clapping their hands. Goodness, what waves there were in that gutter-stream, what rolling tides! It had been a real downpour. The paper boat tossed up and down, sometimes whirling round and round, until the soldier felt quite giddy. But he remained as steadfast as ever, not moving a muscle, still looking straight in front of him, still shouldering arms.

All at once the boat entered a tunnel under the pavement. Oh, it was dark, quite as dark as it was in the box at home. "Wherever am I going now?" the tin soldier wondered. "Yes, it must be the goblin's doing. Ah! If only that young lady were here with me in the boat, I wouldn't care if it were twice as dark."

Suddenly, from its home in the tunnel, out rushed a large water-rat. "Have you a passport?" it demanded. "No entry without a passport!"

But the tin soldier never said a word; he only gripped his musket more tightly than ever. The boat rushed onwards, and behind it rushed the rat in fast pursuit. Ugh! How it ground its teeth, and yelled to the sticks and straws, "Stop him! Stop him! He hasn't paid his toll! He hasn't shown his passport!"

There was no stopping the boat, though, for the stream ran stronger and stronger. The tin soldier could just see a bright glimpse of daylight far ahead where the end of the tunnel must be, but at the same time he heard a roaring noise which well might have frightened a bolder man. Just imagine! At the end of the tunnel the stream thundered down into a great canal. It was as dreadful for him as a plunge down a giant waterfall would be for us.

But how could he stop? Already he was close to the terrible edge. The boat raced on, and the poor tin soldier held himself as stiffly as he could – no one could say of him that he even blinked an eye.

Suddenly the little vessel whirled round three or four times, and filled with water right to the brim; what could it do but sink! The tin soldier stood in water up to his neck; deeper and deeper sank the boat, softer and softer grew the paper, until at last the water closed over the soldier's head. He thought of the lovely little dancer whom he would never see again, and in his ears rang the words of a song:

Onward, onward, warrior brave!
Fear not danger, nor the grave.

Then the paper boat collapsed entirely. Out fell the tin soldier – and he was promptly swallowed up by a fish.

Oh, how dark it was in the fish's stomach! It was even worse than the tunnel, and very much more cramped. But the tin soldier's courage remained unchanged; there he lay, as steadfast as ever, his musket still at his shoulder. The fish swam wildly about, twisted and turned, and then became quite still. Something flashed through like a streak of lightning – then all around was cheerful daylight, and a voice cried out, "The tin soldier!"

The fish had been caught, taken to market, sold and carried into the kitchen, where the cook had cut it open with a large knife. Now she picked up the soldier, holding him round his waist between her finger and thumb, and took him into the living-room, so that all the family could see the remarkable character who had travelled about inside a fish. But the tin soldier was not at all proud. They stood him up on the table, and there – well the world is full of wonders! – he saw that he was in the very same room where his adventures had started; there were the very same children; there were the very same toys; there was the fine paper castle with the graceful little dancer at the door. She was still poised on one leg, with the other raised high in the air. Ah, she was steadfast too.

The tin soldier was deeply moved; he would have liked to weep tin tears, only that would not have been soldierly behaviour. He looked at her, and she looked at him, but not a word passed between them.

And then a strange thing happened. One of the small boys picked up the tin soldier and threw him into the fire. He had no reason for doing this; it must have been the snuff-box goblin's fault.

The tin soldier stood framed in a blaze of light. The heat was intense, but whether this came from the fire or his burning love, he could not tell. His bright colours were now gone – but whether they had been washed away by his journey, or through his grief, none could say. He looked at the pretty little dancer, and she looked at him; he felt that he was melting away, but he still stood steadfast, shouldering arms. Suddenly the door flew open; a gust of air caught the little paper girl, and she flew like a sylph right into the fire, straight to the waiting tin soldier; there she flashed into flame and vanished.

The soldier presently melted down to a lump of tin, and the next day, when the maid raked out the ashes, she found him – in the shape of a little tin heart. And the dancer? All they found was her sequin, and that was as black as soot.

The Jack-in-the-Box

RUTH AINSWORTH

There was once a Jack-in-the-box.
He was a very lively fellow and
all the other toys liked him. His box was
striped red and yellow and when the lid
was lifted and he popped up, he was
dressed in red and yellow too. He always
had a smile on his face.

Inside Jack, under his clothes, was a strong metal spring and it was this that made him jump up so high.

One day, something went wrong. The lid of the box would not open, so Jack could not leap up. This made him very sad. He got bored and cross, shut up in the dark all day and every day. At night he used to cry and his crying kept the other toys awake. He could not sleep himself and they could not sleep either.

"We must do something to help poor Jack-in-the-box," said the other toys. "We must try to make his lid open again so that he can jump out and be happy as he used to be."

"I'll make the lid open," said the hammer from the tool set. "I'm strong. I'll give the lid such a bang that it will fly open."

The hammer had a red handle and a silver head and was very proud of his strength. He gave a great thump on the box, but the lid stayed shut.

"You've made my head ache," said Jack-in-the-box.

"I can do better than that," said the screwdriver. "I can get into cracks. I'll get under the lid and force it open."

The screwdriver got under the lid and began to force it open.

The lid began to crack across the top, but it stayed shut.

"You nearly poked my eye out," grumbled the Jack-in-the-box.

"I'll give him a fright," said the donkey. "I'll creep up to him and then I'll bray loudly. He'll jump with surprise and his head will hit the lid and it will burst open."

The donkey crept quietly across the floor and when he got near the box he brayed his very loudest "hee-haw!"

But nothing happened. The Jack-in-the-box only complained that he was nearly deafened by the noise.

"I have a better plan," said the lion. "I'll roar and pretend I'm going to eat him up. He'll be so frightened and he'll try so hard to get away that he'll burst the box open. You wait and see."

The lion roared so fiercely that all the toys were scared. He sniffed at the box and growled.

"I'm coming to eat you up, Jack-in-the-box. Can you hear me grinding my teeth? You'll make a tasty supper."

"Don't be so stupid," said the Jack-in-the-box. "Even lions can't eat metal springs. Leave me alone."

Now there was a very old monkey who lived in a corner on the top shelf of the toy cupboard. His stuffing was coming out and he had lost an eye. Nobody took much notice of him. But he climbed down from the shelf and said:

"Let me try. I'm not as strong as the hammer or as fierce as the lion, but I've got proper hands and fingers. And although I'm quiet, I do a great deal of thinking in my corner."

"You have only one eye," said the lion.

"But it's a very sharp one," said the monkey. Then very quietly, with no bangs or thumps or roars, he felt the box with his clever fingers and he found a little catch at the side that kept the lid down.

He unfastened the catch and the lid flew up and Jack jumped out, all smiles in his red and yellow coat.

"The catch had stuck," said the monkey. "It's all right now."

The catch never stuck again and Jack could jump up whenever he liked and he always had a special smile for the monkey on the top shelf.

Adventure in the Garden

JOYCE LANKESTER BRISLEY

Once upon a time there were two little wooden dolls, whose names were Purl and Plain.

Purl wore a spotted dress, and Plain wore a plaid one. Otherwise you had to look at them very closely to tell them apart, and then you would notice that Purl's blue-paint eyes were a bit rounder than Plain's, and Plain's wooden nose poked out a bit more than Purl's.

At first sight the two little dolls seemed as if they might be rather prim and proper. But they weren't. They just loved adventures. They were as pleased as anything if they could fall out of the window or into the coal bucket. Once Plain fell into the dustbin, and nearly got carted away with the rubbish. She was rescued only just in time, and had to be washed and set inside the nursery fender to dry; but she was so pleased with herself for having such an adventure that Purl quite wished she had managed to fall in too.

One day Purl and Plain were sitting on the nursery window-sill, with their shiny black heads leaning against the glass, looking out into the garden.

Suddenly Plain said:

"Purl, we're getting stuffy. We need an adventure. Do you know what we'll do?"

"*Ooh*, what, Plain?" said Purl.

"We'll go out there in the Wild, and we'll stay out, all by ourselves, all night!"

Purl knocked her wooden arms excitedly together.

"We will, Plain!" she said. "All by ourselves like real adventurers, and not come back till morning. Do we take luggage?"

"Yes," said Plain. "Tied in bundles in our shawls. That's proper for adventurers. Come on, now. Let's pack up."

So they dropped off the windowsill and ran on their stiff-jointed legs to the nursery cupboard. Plain tossed things about to right and left, till she found two crumpled squares of spotted and plaid stuff, which she dragged from under a box of bricks and spread on the floor. Then Purl solemnly got out a ball, a little box of beads, and a clockwork mouse, and put them on her shawl.

"You don't want things like that out in the Wild!" Plain scoffed. "You want *useful* things. Look, I'll show you!"

So she rummaged about, and brought out two doll's-house cups and plates, a saucepan, a tiny scent bottle (to carry water in, she explained), a pink Christmas candle, and a rather dusty crust of bread.

"All useful things, you see, Purl," said Plain.

"Yes, Plain," said Purl. And she added an elastic band and a piece of string, to show that she understood. (But all the same, while Plain wasn't looking, Purl slipped in her clockwork mouse. So there!)

With their bundles on their backs the two adventurers climbed down mountains of stairs, out into the garden.

"My! What a great place!" said Purl.

"Yes," said Plain. "And there are Wild Animals here – black, and striped, with long tails and claws, that yowl in the night."

"*Ooh!*" shivered Purl.

"But we aren't afraid of them, are we, Plain?"

"Not we! If they come too close we say 'Boo!' and 'Shoo!' – like that – and send them off in a hurry."

The Wild was very beautiful, with nasturtiums and pinks blooming in great clumps beside the path, scenting all the air. Purl stopped to bury her nose in them.

"Come on!" said Plain. "Don't waste time. We've got hundreds of miles to travel before night."

"I was just sucking the honey out," said Purl. "I'm getting hungry."

So Plain stopped to suck honey, too.

And just at that moment there came from away up above them a great, big, growly voice.

"Now then, you! What're you doing on my tidy path?" it said. "You better clear out, or I might sweep you up by mistake, and throw you out on the rubbish heap."

It was a great big Gardener, with a great big broom in his hands.

He didn't look quite like the wild animals Plain had been talking about, but Purl got all ready to say "*Boo!*" and "*Shoo!*" when Plain did. But Plain didn't. She only gave a jump and said "*Ooh!*" in a tiny little voice. And they picked up

their bundles and clattered off down the path in a hurry.

"Why didn't we say '*Boo!*' to him?" asked Purl, when they had got safely away.

"Oh, you never do to Gardeners," said Plain; "only to Wild Animals that yowl in the night."

"Don't Gardeners yowl in the night, Plain?"

"Of course they don't, Purl!"

"How do you know, Plain?"

Plain couldn't think of anything to say to that but "Don't be silly, Purl!" So she said it. And they journeyed on in silence for several miles – until they had crossed the lawn, in fact.

Presently the Wild grew more wild.

There was a rockery to climb, and a high box-hedge to creep through. Then they came to a place where there was a big grey mound where a bonfire had been; and a big hole full of garden rubbish, cabbage leaves, potato peelings, and egg shells; and near it a soft green hill of fine grass cuttings, newly emptied from the lawnmower.

"This is a nice place, Purl," said Plain, looking round. "We could burrow into the grass cuttings to sleep, and wash in the bird bath there in the morning."

"Yes!" said Purl, running to the rubbish-pit. "And look! – little green apples and cabbage leaves, and some teeny-weeny potatoes! There's lots of doll-food here, Plain, and I'm *so* hungry!"

So they got out the doll's-house saucepan and filled it with water from the bird bath. Then they put a tiny potato in, and a piece of cabbage stalk, and bits of egg shell for flavouring, and set the stew on top of the old bonfire to cook, while they spread a shawl for a tablecloth and

set cups and plates on it. They picked nasturtium seeds to mix with little green apples for a tasty dessert.

The stew soon cooked, and smelled very delicious. The dolls were just sniffing at it hungrily, wondering if it were done, when suddenly – there came a rustling in the bushes behind them.

Purl and Plain jumped so that their wooden heads knocked together.

A large striped animal with a long tail and whiskers stared at them with yellow eyes.

"*Mew!*" it said alarmingly.

"*Ooh!*" whispered Purl, "it's a Wild Animal! What do we do now?"

"*B-boo!*" said Plain faintly, waving one arm.

The Wild Animal only stared, swaying the tip of its tail to and fro.

"*Sh-sh-shoo!*" said Plain, more faintly, and not waving.

But the animal only began to step daintily over the egg shells and leaves in the rubbish-pit towards them, to see what was going on.

Purl had a sudden idea. Quickly she got the clockwork mouse from her bundle, wound it up, and set it at the terrifying Wild Animal. The mouse whirred over the ground a little way, then fell on its side, still whirring. But the cat leapt back, and was away behind the bushes in a flash.

"Ha-ha!" said Plain, strutting up and down waving her arms. "We know how to deal with those Wild Animals! They can't scare *us!* — Where did you get that clockwork mouse, Purl?"

"I brought it with me from the toy-cupboard," said Purl firmly, putting it away again. "I thought it might come in useful."

"Well —" said Plain. "Well — let's have supper now. The stew's cooked."

So they gobbled up their supper till there wasn't a bit left. And then they set to work to make a house in the grass-heap.

A cardboard box lid from the rubbish-pit, propped up with twigs, made the roof; grass was piled all over it, and the grass floor scooped out under it, like a cosy nest. And then Purl and Plain, well wrapped in their shawls, crawled in and pulled the grass up over the entrance.

And there they lay, snug as could be, with their crockery and pots safely buried beside them, and the bottle of water, the crust, and the pink Christmas candle handy in case of need. And nobody, not even the Gardener, could possibly have guessed that two little wooden dolls were inside that grass-heap.

They slept all night as sweetly as wooden dolls can sleep. And even though it rained a little in the night they were quite dry when they came home to the nursery after breakfast the next morning.

That was a proper Adventure!

The Tin Horseman

RUSSELL HOBAN

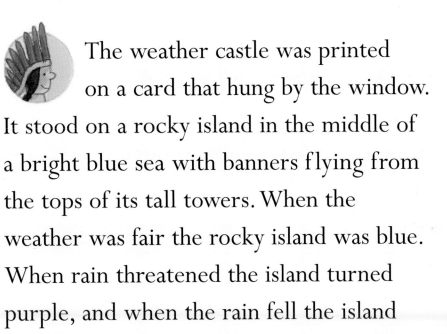

The weather castle was printed on a card that hung by the window. It stood on a rocky island in the middle of a bright blue sea with banners flying from the tops of its tall towers. When the weather was fair the rocky island was blue. When rain threatened the island turned purple, and when the rain fell the island was pink.

The tin horseman lived on a shelf near the window. He had a pale heroic face. He wore a yellow fringed Indian suit and a headdress of red feathers. His dapple-grey horse had a red saddle-cloth. Horse and horseman were a single piece of tin stamped from a mould. They were printed on one side only, the other side was blank. But they were rounded and not flat, and they had feelings.

Long ago there had been a flat tin clown, a red-painted magnet, and two or three coloured rings with the horseman. Now he was alone. Day after day he looked at the little windows of the weather castle, and he was certain that he had seen the face of a beautiful yellow-haired princess at one of them.

"One midnight when the island is blue I shall gallop there and find her," he said. But when the island was blue he did not gallop to the castle, because he was afraid.

The tin horseman was afraid of the round red-and-yellow glass-topped box that was the monkey game of skill. Inside it crouched the monkey, printed on a yellow background. He had a horrid pink face, and empty holes where his eyes belonged. His eyes were silver balls that had to be shaken into place.

The tin horseman was afraid that when the monkey had his eyes in place he might do dreadful things, and he was sure that the monkey was skilful enough to shake them into place whenever he wanted to. The monkey lived between the tin horseman and the castle, and the tin horseman never dared to gallop past.

Day after day he looked at the castle windows, and daily he became more certain that he saw the yellow-haired princess. Once he thought she even waved her hand to him. "When the island is pink I shall gallop there," he said. "One rainy midnight I shall smash the glass and throw away the monkey's silver eyes and ride to the princess." But he was afraid, and stayed where he was, dusty on the shelf.

One night, just between midnight and the twelve strokes of the clock, words came to the tin horseman: "Now or never." He didn't know whether he had heard them or thought them, but his fear left him, and in the dim light from the window he spurred his horse toward the weather castle and the princess of his dream.

now or never...

Just as he was passing the monkey game of skill he was surrounded by complete darkness. All was black, and he could see nothing. Again words came to him:

"Fear is blind, but courage gives me eyes."

And again the tin horseman did not know where the words came from nor why he did what he did next.

He dismounted, and felt in the dark for the monkey game of skill. He remembered his thought of smashing the glass and throwing away the eyes, but he did not do that. He shook it gently. One, two, he heard the eyes roll into place. He closed his eyes and waited.

A golden glow came from the glass top of the box, and seeing the glow through his closed eyelids he opened his eyes. The monkey was gone. There in the golden light stood the yellow-haired princess he had longed for. She was not in the weather castle, but here before him.

"Your courage has broken my enchantment," she said. "There is a sorcerer who lives in the weather castle. It was he who wanted you to smash the glass and throw away the monkey's eyes, and if you had done that I should have been lost to you for ever."

"Now I *will* ride to the castle," said the tin horseman. He pried the glass top off the box and took the princess up on his horse.

Over the blue sea they galloped, straight to the island and up the great stone steps to the castle. The castle was empty. The sorcerer had fled.

After that the tin horseman and the princess lived in the weather castle with the banners flying from the towers, while the island turned blue or pink or purple as the weather changed.

But the glass was back on top of the red-and-yellow box that had been the monkey game of skill. From then on someone else lived there, and no one ever looked to see who it might be.

The Little Girl and the Tiny Doll

AINGELDA ARDIZZONE

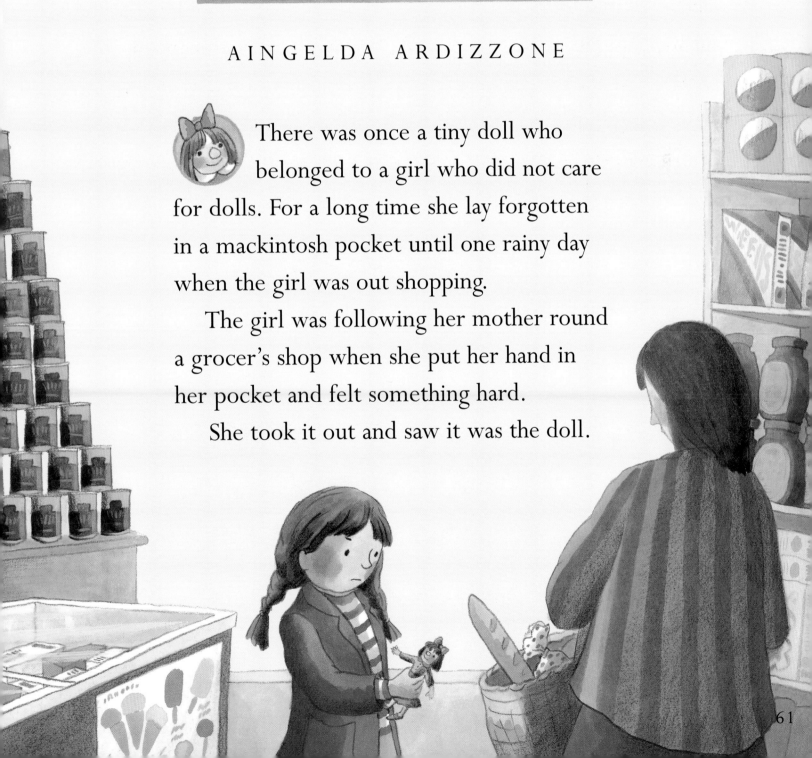 There was once a tiny doll who belonged to a girl who did not care for dolls. For a long time she lay forgotten in a mackintosh pocket until one rainy day when the girl was out shopping.

The girl was following her mother round a grocer's shop when she put her hand in her pocket and felt something hard.

She took it out and saw it was the doll.

"Ugly old thing," she said and quickly put it back again, as she thought, into her pocket. But, in fact, since she didn't want the doll, she dropped it unnoticed into the deep-freeze among the frozen peas.

The tiny doll lay quite still for a long time, wondering what was to become of her. She felt so sad, partly because she did not like being called ugly and partly because she was lost.

It was very cold in the deep-freeze and the tiny doll began to feel rather stiff, so she decided to walk about and have a good look at the place. The floor was crisp and white just like frost on a winter's morning. There were many packets of peas piled one on top of the other. They seemed to her like great big buildings. The cracks between the piles were rather like narrow streets.

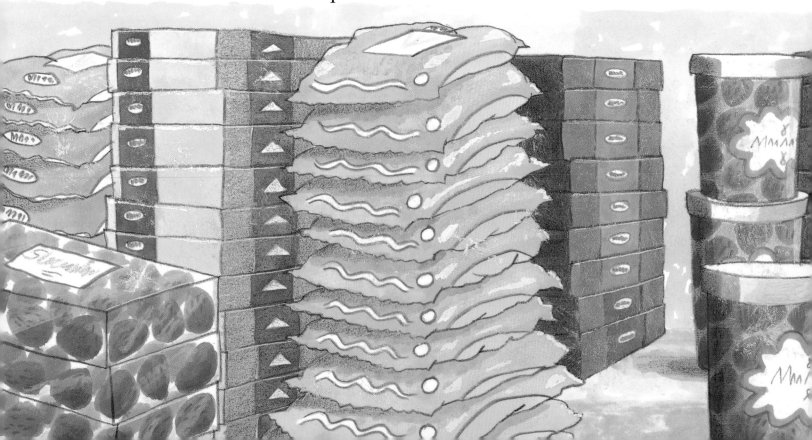

She walked one way and then the other, passing not only packets of peas, but packets of sliced beans, spinach, broccoli and mixed vegetables. Then she turned a corner and found herself among beef rissoles and fish fingers. However, she did not stop but went on exploring until she came to boxes of strawberries; and then ice cream. The strawberries reminded her of the time when she was lost once before among the strawberry plants in a garden. Then she sat all day in the sun smelling and eating strawberries.

Now she made herself as comfortable as possible among the boxes. The only trouble was that people were continually taking boxes out to buy them and the shop people were always putting in new ones. At times it was very frightening. Once she was nearly squashed by a box of fish fingers.

The tiny doll had no idea how long she spent in the deep-freeze. Sometimes it seemed very quiet. This, she supposed, was when the shop was closed for the night.

She could not keep count of the days.

One day when she was busy eating ice cream out of a packet, she suddenly looked up and saw a little girl she had never seen before.

The little girl was sorry for the tiny doll and wished she could take her home.

The doll looked so cold and lonely, but the girl did not dare to pick her up because she had been told not to touch things in the shop. However, she felt she must do something to help the doll and as soon as she got home she set to work to make her some warm clothes.

First of all, she made her a warm bonnet out of a piece of red flannel.

This was a nice and easy thing to start with.

After tea that day she asked her mother to help her cut out a coat from a piece of blue velvet.

She stitched away so hard that she had just time to finish it before she went to bed.

It was very beautiful.

The next day her mother said they were going shopping, so the little girl put the coat and bonnet in an empty matchbox and tied it into a neat parcel with brown paper and string. She held the parcel tightly in her hand as she walked along the street. As soon as she reached the shop she ran straight to the deep-freeze to look for the tiny doll. At first she could not see her anywhere. Then, suddenly, she saw her, right at the back, playing with the peas. The tiny doll was throwing them into the air and hitting them with an ice cream spoon. The little girl threw in the parcel

and the doll at once started to untie it. She looked very pleased when she saw what was inside. She tried on the coat, and it fitted. She tried on the bonnet and it fitted too. She jumped up and down with excitement and waved to the little girl to say thank you. She felt so much better in warm clothes and it made her feel happy to think that somebody cared for her.

Then she had an idea. She made the matchbox into a bed and pretended that the brown paper was a great big blanket. With the string she wove a mat to go beside the bed.

At last she settled down in the matchbox, wrapped herself in the brown paper blanket and went to sleep. She had a long, long sleep because she was very tired and, when she woke up, she found that the little girl had been back again and had left another parcel. This time it contained a yellow scarf.

Now the little girl came back to the shop every day and each time she brought something new for the tiny doll. She made her a sweater, a petticoat, knickers with tiny frills, and gave her a little bit of looking-glass to see herself in. She also gave her some red tights which belonged to one of her own dolls to see if they would fit. They fitted perfectly. At last the tiny doll was beautifully dressed and looked quite cheerful, but still nobody except the little girl ever noticed her.

"Couldn't we ask someone about the doll?" the little girl asked her mother. "I would love to take her home to play with."

The mother said she would ask the lady at the cash desk when they went to pay for their shopping.

"Do you know about the doll in the deep-freeze."

"No, indeed," the lady replied. "There are no dolls in this shop."

"Oh yes, there are," said the little girl and her mother, both at once. So the lady from the cash desk, the little girl and her mother all marched off to have a look. And there, sure enough, was the tiny doll down among the frozen peas.

"It's not much of a life for a doll in there," said the shop lady, picking up the doll and giving it to the little girl. "You had better take her home where she will be out of mischief." Having said this, she marched back to her desk with rather a haughty expression.

The little girl took the tiny doll home, where she lived for many happy years in a beautiful doll's house. The little girl played with her a great deal, but, best of all, she liked the company of the other dolls. They all loved to listen to her adventures in the deep-freeze.

The Nutcracker

E. T. A. HOFFMANN

RETOLD BY VIVIAN FRENCH

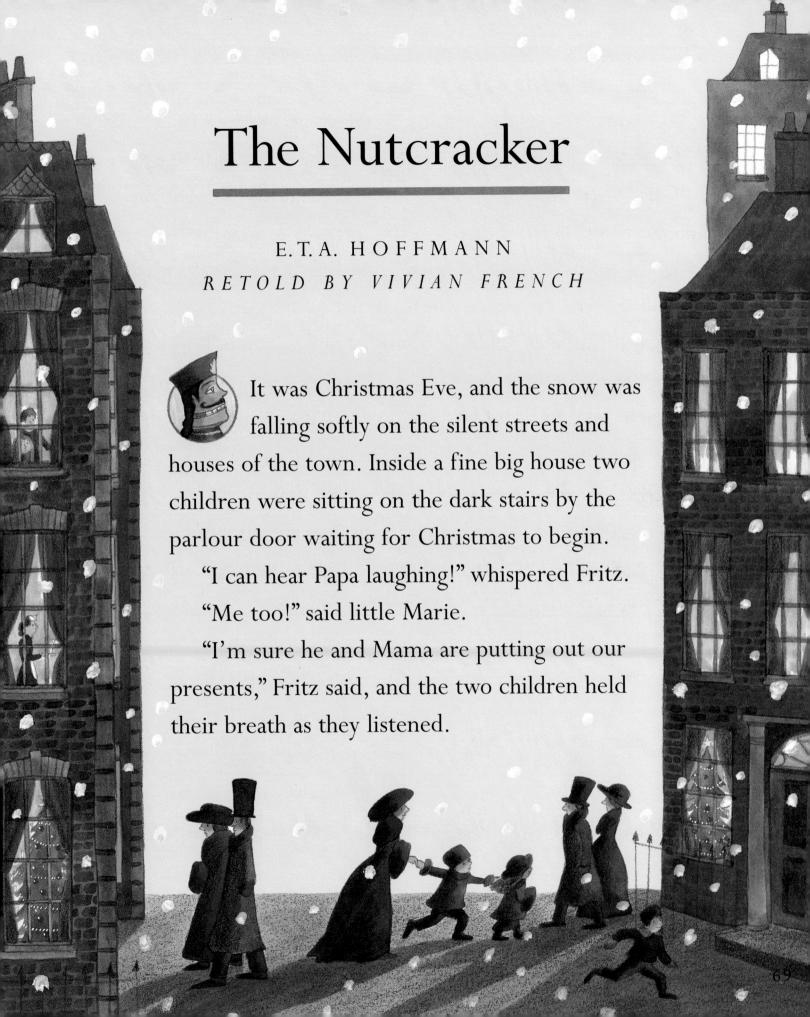 It was Christmas Eve, and the snow was falling softly on the silent streets and houses of the town. Inside a fine big house two children were sitting on the dark stairs by the parlour door waiting for Christmas to begin.

"I can hear Papa laughing!" whispered Fritz.

"Me too!" said little Marie.

"I'm sure he and Mama are putting out our presents," Fritz said, and the two children held their breath as they listened.

Fritz was quite right. On the other side of the parlour door Papa was busy arranging all the presents, and Mama was busy lighting the candles on the Christmas tree so that they shone like tiny glittering stars.

Behind a pile of picture books stood something very special. It was not a doll, or a teddy bear, or a wooden horse – it was a nutcracker. His head was big, and his body was small, but he was very handsome – for a nutcracker. He wore a shiny red coat, his hair was tied in a pigtail, and his teeth were white and strong. If you put a nut into his mouth and pulled on his pigtail then CRACK! the shell fell neatly into pieces. He was a truly wonderful cracker of nuts, and – even more wonderful – he had a secret . . .

Once upon a time Nutcracker had been a boy, a real, live boy, with a fine red coat and a pigtail. What was more, he loved to show pretty girls how he could crack a nut with his strong white teeth. But one terrible day the wicked Queen of the Mice had put a spell on him, and turned him into a nutcracker. The spell was so strong that it could only be broken if someone could love Nutcracker just as he was, with his big head and his small body.

Now poor Nutcracker stood stiffly under the Christmas tree. He had heard that a little girl lived in the house, and he was hoping and hoping that she would find him and love him. If she did, then maybe the terrible spell would be broken and he would be a boy again.

At last everything in the parlour was ready. Papa put the last soldier straight, and the doors were flung wide open. Fritz and Marie ran in – and stopped to stare and stare at all the toys and dolls and soldiers and pretty things. Nutcracker hardly dared to breathe. Would the little girl see him? Would she like him? Would she love him?

Fritz began to march his soldiers up and down. Marie looked at the dolls, and then ran to choose a book from under the tree – but suddenly she stopped quite still.

"OH!" Marie's eyes opened wide. "What a strange little wooden man." She picked up Nutcracker. "Oh, he has such a beautiful smile!"

At once Fritz came running over. "Let me see! Why, it's a nutcracker! Let me try him! Here's a nut – and another! And a big one—"   C R A C K !

"Be careful, Fritz!" said Marie, but she was too late. Fritz had given Nutcracker such a huge nut to crack that his teeth were bent and broken. Marie snatched him up, and wrapped him in a handkerchief.

"Don't worry, dear Nutcracker," she said. "I will look after you."

That night Marie was the last to leave the parlour. She was tenderly tucking Nutcracker up in one of her doll's beds in a cupboard when she heard a tiny noise.

Scritch! Scritch! Scritch!

Marie turned round to see what the noise could be. It came again, a little louder.

Scratch! Scratch! Scratch!

Marie's heart went pitter patter. What could it be? She looked all around, but still she could see nothing. Then –

"SQUEAK! SQUEAK! SQUEAK!" An army of mice came running into the room. In the lead was the biggest mouse Marie had ever seen, and on his head were seven crowns.

"Oh! Oh! OH!" Marie began to tremble.

Inside the cupboard Nutcracker jumped up. He knew at once that this was the King of the Mice – the son of his enemy, the Queen.

"Dear Marie!" he called. "Don't be frightened!" He seized a sword from one of Fritz's toy soldiers, and waved it in the air.

The toy soldiers leapt up out of their boxes, and the tin elephant blew on his trumpet.

TOOT! TOOT! TOOOOOOT!

Nutcracker and the soldiers marched out of the cupboard. The mice dashed at them, and Nutcracker waved his sword once more.

"Who will help us?" he called, and at once all the stuffed toys and the dolls and the gingerbread men and the gingerbread women

and the pink sugar mice and the marzipan pigs ran out to help.

BANG! CRASH! ROLY-POLY THUMP!

The soldiers fired pop guns and the teddy bears rolled skittles.
The sailor dolls swung down on ropes, and the clockwork
clown juggled oranges and lemons as she rolled into battle.
The smiley clown helped the marzipan pigs toss wooden beads at
the enemy, and the gingerbread men and women ran here and
there, helping the toys that fell this way and that. The tin elephant
trundled round and round and round, TOOT TOOT TOOTING
as he went, and many of the mice squeaked loudly as he ran over
their toes.

It was a long hard battle –
and there were bumps and
bruises all round. At last
Nutcracker jumped up into the
air – and DOWN on the Mouse
King's tail.
"EEEEEEEKKKKKK!"
The Mouse King vanished, and
only his seven golden crowns were
left, rolling on the carpet. Bowing
low, Nutcracker picked them up and presented them to Marie.

"Thank you, thank you, dear Nutcracker," said Marie. "Thank
you for saving me from those
horrible mice!"

Nutcracker bowed again.
"Dear Marie," he said,
"let me take you on a
journey. Let me show you
the magical land where I
have been living, the
magical land behind the
cupboard . . ."

And that's exactly where they went. A little staircase led up through the cupboard doors to the most wonderful place Marie had ever seen. They walked slowly through Candy Meadow and past the Almond and Raisin Gate, through Christmas Forest and down to the Orangewater Brook.

"It leads to the Lemonade River, you know," said Nutcracker, and he led Marie a little further down to Lake Rosa. There they stepped into a little shell boat pulled by two golden dolphins, and away they sailed to Jelly and Jam Grove. As the boat skimmed over the sweet-smelling waves, Nutcracker told Marie the story of the spell the Queen of the Mice had put on him.

When he had finished, Nutcracker sighed, and a silver tear rolled down his wooden face. Marie silently took his hand.

BUMP! Just at that moment the little boat bumped into the shore of Jelly and Jam Grove, and at once Nutcracker cheered up.

"Come, dear Marie," he said, and he helped her out of the boat.

On and on Marie and Nutcracker wandered, past spun sugar trees and sparkling crystal oranges and shining spiced lemons . . . until at last they came to Marzipan Castle, where four little princesses ran to Nutcracker and hugged him and patted him and called him Brother.

"So you must be a prince, dear Nutcracker!" Marie said.

Nutcracker bowed.

Marie curtsied back, and felt herself spinning and spinning and spinning . . . and she closed her eyes.

When Marie opened her eyes again she was in her own bed, and her mother was beside her.

"Christmas Day!" said Mama. "Hurry! Your godfather will be here very soon."

"Oh, Mama!" said Marie. "I have been to such a beautiful, beautiful place!" – but no one would believe her when she told them all the wonderful things she had seen.

At last Marie went slowly and sadly out of the room and into the parlour . . . and there in the cupboard was Nutcracker, looking as wooden as could be.

Marie gazed at him. "Dear Nutcracker," she said. "You were so brave, fighting the King of the Mice. And you showed me such wonderful things . . . even if it was only a dream. If you really were alive, I'd never send you away. I'd love you for ever and ever."

TANTARRA! TANTARRA!

What was that? Marie was quite sure that she had heard trumpets . . . but where was her dear Nutcracker? She rubbed her eyes. He was no longer in the cupboard! And who was that coming through the door?

"My dear Marie," said her godfather. "I am so happy – so VERY happy – to be able to introduce you to my nephew. And he smiled and smiled as a handsome boy in a fine red coat bowed low and took Marie's hand . . . and cracked a nut with his strong white teeth.